Welcome to Camp Croak!

www.guppybooks.co.uk

GHOUL SCOUTS

Welcome to Camp Croak!

taylor dolan

GUPPY
BOOKS

Mom, thank you for being the "YAY" to my "BOO". I wish more folks were as genuinely kind as you are, it would be a much better world. Dad, thank you for thinking Ghoul Scouts was a good idea even when it wasn't. And for getting us a dog, even though you have allergies. You are lovely. Ness, thank you for bringing so much joy and laughter to everything you do, and for teaching me with true patience. Bella, thank you for changing my life and taking on this zany story. And Pam, thank you for being you. I can't wait to read the next beautiful, creepy book you make.

GHOUL SCOUTS: WELCOME TO CAMP CROAK!
is a GUPPY BOOK

First published in the UK in 2020 by
Guppy Books
Bracken Hill
Cotswold Road
Oxford OX2 9JG

Text and illustrations © Taylor Dolan, 2020
Cover and insides designed by Ness Wood

978 1 913101 06 0

1 3 5 7 9 10 8 6 4 2

The rights of Taylor Dolan to be identified as the author and illustrator of this work
have been asserted in accordance with the Copyright, Designs and Patents Act 1988.

Papers used by Guppy Books are from well-managed forests
and other responsible sources.

MIX
Paper from
responsible sources
FSC® C017574
FSC
www.fsc.org

GUPPY PUBLISHING LTD Reg. No. 11565833

A CIP catalogue record for this book is available from the British Library.

Typeset in 15/26pt ITC Clearface by Falcon Oast Graphic Art Ltd.
Printed and bound in UK

For my sissy, Lexie.
I was going to name the main character Lemon,
but my editor thought it sounded a little
too weird. So, I stole your name instead.

chapter one

THE SKELETON IN MY CLOSET

If you're getting ready to read this book – even after looking at the title and the real weird cover drawings – then you just *might* be ready for the truth.

Grams says I have to stress the word *might*, as I have seen a fair few

folks pick up my book, panic, and run away flapping like headless chickens.

Grown-ups are the worst for it. The older you are, the more scared you get of *everything*. It's a fact of life. And let me tell you something they don't want us to know. Grown-ups are scared

ALL. THE. TIME.

That's why their hair is grey and they get all them face wrinkles. It's all that *scared* drying them up from the inside out, like a prune.

They are terrified the perfectly good chocolate chunk cookie that just fell on the bathroom floor is now full of deadly germs.

GERMS

CHOCOLATE?
NOPE.
still germs.

Worried that other grown-ups sit around judging them at dinner parties they weren't invited to.

They are even afraid that when they go away for the weekend, they might experience a 'worst case scenario'. Watch a grown-up next time they are chucking stuff in a suitcase, you'll see. Nobody needs ten pairs of underwear for a three-day trip.

This book is not for them. It's for people like YOU. People who might look ordinary from the outside, but have something special burbling up beneath their skin. You don't have to

THE BRAVERY X-RAY

be brave, you just have to *want* to be brave. That's half the battle fought, right there.

So here it is. Take a deep breath, sit down and maybe put on some of that calming music, because it's honest-to-goodness genuine truth time and the things you don't know could probably fill a whole museum.

GHOSTS
are
REAL.

Same as vampires, chupacabras, radish monsters, sea beasties, swamp ghouls and Bigfoot. I swear on the life of my Grams and her five fat cats, I am telling you the whole truth.

After all, I should know.

My

best friend

is

A WEREWOLF.

Chapter two

NOT ALL THOSE WHO WANDER ARE LOST, ESPECIALLY IF THEY BROUGHT GPS

My Grams always told me that on those days when the whole world seems a bit more bonkers than normal: look around you and count the facts. Facts help a person keep their feet on the ground.

My name is Lexie. It's short for Alexandra, but don't even think about calling me that. You can also call me the very best number one storyteller in Shreveport, I got me a ribbon to prove it.

FACT No 2

My Grams is the best person in the whole wide world. Even if her house  smells like cat pee. You might think this is an opinion, but I'm saying it's a fact. So there.

FACT No 3

Somehow, something went very wrong this morning.

Maybe it was my fault for reading in the car when I was supposed to be Map Captain. Or maybe it happened when me and Grams got really into singing Dolly Parton and neither of us noticed the big ol' warning sign. Whoever's fault it was, we definitely took a wrong turn somewhere.

And now, I am standing *here*. All by myself. Having a sneaky suspicion. And that sneaky suspicion is making my face sweat and my stomach feel like it is full of evil butterflies.

I think Grams has dropped me off at the wrong summer camp . . .

DANGER.
DANGER?
DANGER!

chapter three

BE CAREFUL WHAT YOU WITCH FOR

Originally, she signed me up for a place called 'The Happy Hollow Camp for Joyful Boys and Girls'.

Ew. Double Ew.

I didn't tell Grams, because I would never do anything to hurt her feelings,

but honestly, those pictures made me feel real sick inside.

I do not have giant white teeth. I do not like sports that bounce. And I certainly do not want to sleep in a cabin that looks like the candy house from Hansel and Gretel.

I was definitely *not* looking forward to that camp, but I am not so sure that this one is any better.

Then I noticed someone coming out of the dark patch of trees. Someone who looked like a Scout Leader with one teensy difference.

"You are late, Miss Wilde, lateness is
not to be tolerated!" frowned one head.

"Hush and shush, Parsleigh, fifteen
seconds is hardly a hanging offence,
now, is it?" grinned the middle head.

"Welcome to Camp Munster, Lexie,"
beamed the third and final head as she

said my name that I had definitely *not* already told her. "Hop on and we'll get you settled in with the other Ghoul Scouts in no time at all!"

And then, they handed me a broom . . .

And just like that, I knew I was about to do something real silly 'cause a bunch of imaginary warning bells started jangling in my head. My sneaky uncomfortable suspicion had been SUPER right.

This is *not* the Happy Hollow Camp for Joyful Boys and Girls.

And I think my new Troop Leaders just might be . . .

WITCHES.

Giddy-up, I guess?

chapter four

NOT JUST LIKE RIDING A BIKE

AAAAHHH
HHHHHHHH
HHHHHHHHH

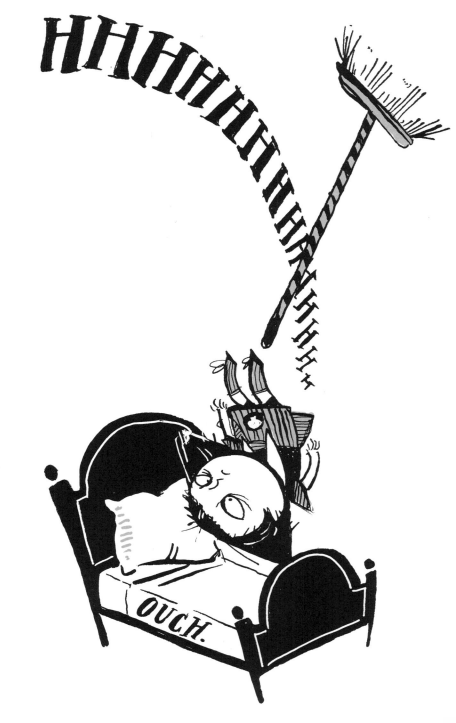

chapter five

TASTES JUST LIKE CHICKEN

W ell, I can honestly say, I never thought I would be the type to faint from being afraid. But then again, I never thought I would be the type to ride a household cleaning implement over dark swamps. So I guess we learn something new about ourselves every day.

I was just brushing myself off, and getting my breath back, when I saw a tiny note on the pillow next to me.

Wer would be delighted to have you for dinner, sweetie. If you wake up in time, head on over to the bonfire and we'll get cooking! Sincerely, The Sisters (Miss Parsleigh, Miss Sage and Miss Rosemarie)

Wait. Wait, just a very long minute.

I looked at the little piece of paper again, and this time focused on the problem words. 'We would be delighted to **HAVE YOU FOR DINNER.**'

Oh no. NOOOOO, ma'am.

This is just awful news! I have ridden a broom straight into a camp of folks who want to eat me for dinner!

You know what, again I say,
NO.

Besides, I would be a terrible main course! I'm such a tiny little girl. At best, I'm snack-sized. Like those mini candy bars the cheap houses give away on Halloween. Nobody gets full on a fun-sized candy bar.

As much as I was hoping that I would never have to fly again,

I'm not sticking around here long enough to get turned into a deep-fried people taco!

But just as I was gearing myself up for flight *numero dos*, I heard a strange snuffly sound coming from across the room . . .

chapter six

SPEAK SOFTLY AND CARRY A BIG BROOM

N ow there are three ways a smarty, like myself, can use a broom.

1. As a cleaning implement to get up dust and cat hair from the kitchen floor.

 **2.** As a flying vehicle that goes fast and makes me want to keel over.

3. And most importantly, in this highly dangerous situation, as a poking stick to keep people-eaters away from me.

I grabbed my poking stick and hollered, "HEY! Listen up, there will be no little girl gumbo for you tonight, mister! So you just show yourself nice and slow, and keep your hands where I can see 'em."

They always say that in Grams'
favourite detective programmes, and it
made me feel a little more official.

I was ready to *jabjabjab* some evil-
looking bayou cannibal man with a
wicked squint that says, "I bet I can
get a few days' leftovers outta her . . ."

I was *not* ready for who actually stood up.

"P-p-please don't poke me, little girl gumbo is not on the menu. I'm begging you, hush up a bit. Loud noises make me real nervous, and I, I . . . I'm already nervous to begin with."

She was gulping down air like a land-stuck fish.

Oh fudge, this is not the time for a poking stick! It's the time for kindness and a little distraction. I remember Dad having these kind of dark days before I went to live with Grams. I put down the broom slowly, and plopped quietly next to her.

"Look, I'm real sorry, honest. Guess I was being a teensy bit oversensitive about the cannibalism thing. But now that I know I'm not for supper, how's about I tell you a story? After all, bet you didn't know that you happen to be sitting next to Lexie Wilde, the very best number one storyteller in all of Shreveport."

She didn't tell me to shut up, so I took that as my sign for story time.

"Once upon a time there was a fabulous young coyote named Juan Fernando who had dreams of becoming a professional yodeller. The other coyotes thought this was the most foolish thing they had ever heard. And each night, when the moon would rise, they would go, 'AWOOOOO!' or 'AWOOOO — hahaha, Juan Fernando is a loser.'

"They were very
rude. But Juan Fernando,
he did not care. When he
saw the moon, he would take a
deep happy breath and go, 'Yodel-
Ay-Ee-Oooo0000,' instead."

I yodelled real loud, and my new
friend cracked a smile. I could see that
my distraction was working.

"And when the full moon filled the
sky like a golden pancake he would sing,
**'Ahl-dee-oh-lay-hee-hee,
Oh-dah-lay-hee-hee,
Oh-dah-lay-heeeeeeeeee.'**"

Well, my yodelling must've been
something terrible, because she burst

into a fit of giggles. And then, much to my surprise, she burst into something else completely.

"Fun fact about werewolves," she sighed happily. "The moon don't do nothing for us at all, but

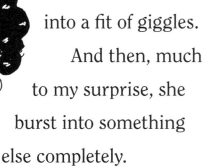

sometimes when we get the jitters, POOF, back to being all human. Happens to the best of us."

And she smiled at me with a full row of bright sharp teeth.

chapter seven

DON'T JUDGE A WEREWOLF BY HER COVER

I was collecting my thoughts and picking my jaw up off of the floor when the front door of the cabin opened with a bang.

"Emmy LouLou, no offence, but you look like Auntie Arsene last time she done crawled out of her grave, you."

All this was said in a rush of Creole confidence from a puffed-up skeleton whose hair was alive with electricity.

"Who dat girl dere?" And she pointed her bony finger right at *me*.

"Be nice, Bébé," hiccuped Emmy LouLou. She dabbed her puffy eyes with her paw. "I don't think we need to get rid of this one. Her name's Lexie, she's got a gift with words."

"Mmhmm." Bébé eyeballed me before sticking out her hand. "The name's Bébé, like she said, pronounced Bay-Bay cause it's French, ya hear? I am the adopted daughter of the Voodoo Loa his self, Baron Samedi. So long as we stay friends, you ain't got nothing to worry about, *cher*."

I vaguely remember my Grams telling me a story about Baron Samedi. He is the Voodoo spirit of cemeteries and death, so if

the Baron decided to use his powers to keep *this* girl around, well, I ain't gonna be the one to make her mad. So I shook her hand and tried not to look jumpy when her finger bones rattled.

She gestured over her shoulder to a ghost in a baseball cap. (Yes, I said ghost, you've met a talking skeleton and a werewolf already – time we get with the programme, y'all.)

"This cutie pie is Sweet Boo. She don't say much, but that don't mean she ain't got a world of things going on in that floaty head of hers."

Sweet Boo giggled, and continued to bounce like a happy dead marshmallow.

Just when I was thinking my quota of surprises for the day had reached its super limit, one final shape stepped forward out from the shadows.

"I would shake your hand, but I seem to have lost it. My hand that is. It's as lost as your inside voice. We heard you yodelling a mile away."

I've never met a zombie before, but I have to say, I didn't expect her to sound like a Mary Poppins robot.

"I'm Mary Shelley. You may call me Mary, or Mary Shelley. If you feel the need to give me a nickname, find something else to do with your time."

"Nice to meet you, Mary Shelley," I said and smiled at her.

"So what is *you*, anyways?" Bébé butted in. "If you ended up at this camp, you gotta *be* something. You is pretty pale, but you ain't no vampire, that's fo' sure."

"You got me there," I had to admit. "I'm not a vampire, but I am the very best number one storyteller in Shreveport – that has to count for something, right?"

"Mmmhmmm," tsked Bébé, slowly eyeballing me one final time.

Guess I must have passed some secret Ghoul Scout test because just like that, she turned away and started getting ready for bed.

A few hours later, as I was listening to Emmy LouLou growl in the bed next to me, I realized that there must be so many things I don't know anything about in this big ol' world of ours. What I *do* know is – this is either going to

be the very best,
most interesting
summer that ever
happened, or I am
in **deep doodoo.**

chapter eight

HOW TO CATCH A COLD

I woke up from a dead sleep and near jumped out of my skin when a crackling voice came singing out over the intercom in our cabin.

"Happy Midnight, my dear Boos and Ghouls! Listen to the cicadas scream and 'gators sing. Let that humidity wrap around you like a damp washcloth, 'cause it's time to play your favourite game, 'How to Catch a Cold'. So wiggle those toesies into some boots and let's get going!"

Ew, wait – what?

I hate having colds, why would I go out and catch one on purpose? I don't think I'm being goofy here by saying that a cold is not a thing most people want to have. A whole entire cake, or reading an amazing book and then finding out it's a series –

those are things most people want.

However, I have always been a team player so I pulled on my boots and joined the others outside. We could barely see our own noses through the fog (well, those of us who have noses), but somehow we made our way to the swamp edge where the Sisters were waiting for us.

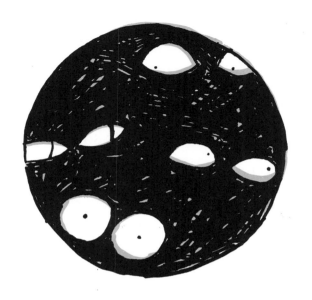

"Alrighty, my twisted friends, we
got us an infestation on our hands.
So many glorious sicknesses to catch!
Team Bones is gonna be Emmy
LouLou, Bébé and Lexie. That means
Team Skins is Sweet Boo, Mary and
us," crowed Miss Sage.

Sweet Boo and Mary broke away
excitedly and started rifling through a
pile of old jam jars and butterfly nets
that I hadn't noticed before. Guess my
eyes were still adjusting to the dark.

Emmy LouLou leaned in and patted
my shoulder. "Why don't you be the
Sneezer, since this is your first time?
It's a real easy game
once you get the hang
of it. That leaves me
and Bébé to be the
Snatchers."

Bébé opened
her mouth
to protest.

Clearly she was not happy about being a Snatcher, whatever that was, but she got cut off like a whip crack by Miss Parsleigh.

"Now, you best show respect, Bébé," huffed Miss Parsleigh. "I love me some spirit, Hades knows I do, but you don't get to be Sneezer every time. Teamwork cannot be spelled without the word 'meat', and you will be dead meat, missy, if you don't learn to share at least once a month."

I looked over at Team Skins, hoping that I might get some sort of idea in my head how to play this game of theirs.

Nope, not a darn clue.

I turned around to ask Emmy LouLou to fill me in.

When, suddenly, with a trumpeting elephant loudness, the Sisters hollered, "ON YOUR MARKS, GET SET, SNEEZE!"

chapter nine

SICK AS A DOG

And just like that, Mary started rolling around on the ground, holding her nose and hollering.

"ACHOO! The *Merriam Webster Dictionary* says that the common cold

is 'an acute disease of the
upper respiratory tract'.
I feel the inflammation
of my mucus
membranes moving
from my nose, throat,
eyes and even eustachian
tubes . . .
ACHOO!"
I was just about to
run back to the cabin
to call for a doctor when something
truly amazing happened. The swamp

started lighting up with hundreds of strange sickly green blobs. Like fireflies. Only blobbier and greener and much, much bigger. (So not really like fireflies, I guess.)

They floated closer to Mary every time she yelled about her mucus membranes. When the blobs got close enough, Sweet Boo and the Sisters started plucking them blobs out of the air with their butterfly nets and stuffing what they caught into a bunch of jars.

"UGH, get a move on, Sneezer!" stomped Bébé at me. "Team Skins is gonna catch all the good ones!"

"You can do it, Lex, look at what Mary is doing. You just pretend to be sick as a dog, and use that word gift of yours," whispered Emmy LouLou.

She had nice eyes, they had some real kindness in them, so I nodded that I understood, even if I didn't understand all the way.

"Something is fearfully wrong with me!

ACHOO!" I
spluttered
out. And lo and
behold, as soon as I fake-sneezed, the
blobs stopped their blobbing and just
hovered. Hovered like maybe they
had ears hidden in their goo and were
listening to see if I was
worth a quick
investigation.

I doubled over, and dropped to my knees. "My very bones are riddled with sickness. I can feel the hair falling off my head, and my nose growing larger by the second. Oh my heart, oh my pimples, why do you hurt me so?" I started hacking up a lung, coughing like an old smoker.

I got a snort of laughter from Emmy LouLou (and even a tiny smile from Bébé, A++ for me!) as they began gleefully snatching blob after blob from the sky. Cause you better believe, them blobs were now zooming our way like sideways fireworks.

I opened my mouth to groan again,

when I glanced over at Mary. She was struggling to find more new words and her ears were turning embarrassed red.

I knew what needed doing.

"Sweet Mary!" I reached out, hands a-trembling. "I think today is the day we die. We are clearly BOTH so very sick. I can see the purple sweat on your forehead, which is never a good sign." I began crawling towards her.

Mary looked confused, until I winked at her at least five times and mouthed, "Let's do this *together*."

"OH! Yes, the sweat. The . . . uh . . . *purple* sweat of sickness is on my face and body?" *DING DING DING*, she had caught on.

"And your toenails, have they started to fall off yet? I can feel mine wiggling apart as I say my final words to you." I shook my boots, and her eyes widened as she tried to swallow down

a laugh. There were now plenty of blobs to go round, and all the Snatchers were having a ball.

"Yes! Yes! My toenails, the fungal infection has set in. And . . . OH. MY. HADES!" She waved her stump in the air, and wailed banshee style. "WHERE IS MY LEG? MY WHOLE LEG HAS DISAPPEARED FROM AN ABSOLUTELY RANDOM DISEASE WHICH CERTAINLY HAS NOTHING WHATSOEVER

TO DO WITH ME BEING BORN
THIS WAY!"

The final two blobs were making
their last stand, and without any
words Teams Skins and Bones
officially joined together.

"Goodbye, cruel world," I gasped.
"You may take our legs and our
toenails. You may give us painful
spots, but we'll always have Paris."
(I heard that last part in a movie. It
was a black-and-white film so I knew
it was a solid, famous, last words kinda
line.) With that, Mary and I splatted
flat on the ground, and our friends
done snatched themselves every

single
not-firefly
stubborn
blob.
    We had our
jars and we had our
nets. But most
importantly,
**we had
each other.**

chapter ten

TIME FLIES LIKE A RABID BAT WHEN YOU'RE HAVING FUN

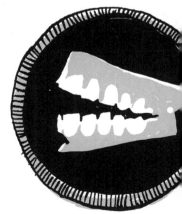

Holy Crow! This camp is better than butter on fresh cornbread! I imagine it's exactly the same as a real Girl Scout Camp, but none of their

campers are dead and they don't get to earn all the weird badges. I have learned so many useful things here, and I thought I was doing alright on being smart.

We take turns at Camp Croak: one badge challenge picked by one camper, every day.

First was Sweet Boo's turn: she chose Fire Safety.

Next, Mary chose
Needlecraft, and was kind
enough to let all of us practise
on some spare limbs she found
in her bedside table.

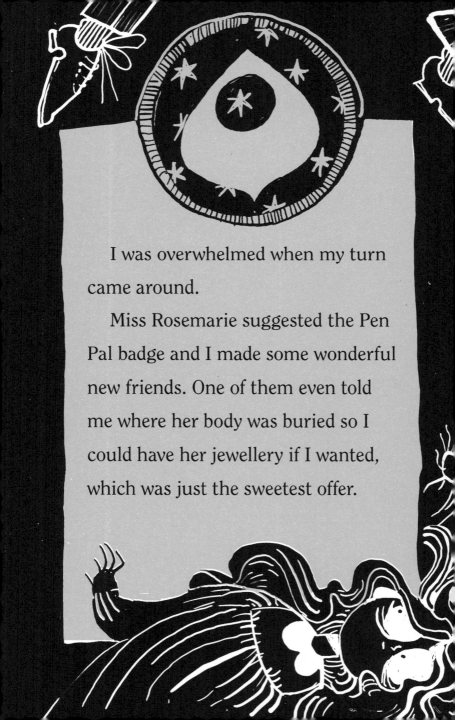

I was overwhelmed when my turn came around.

Miss Rosemarie suggested the Pen Pal badge and I made some wonderful new friends. One of them even told me where her body was buried so I could have her jewellery if I wanted, which was just the sweetest offer.

Bébé was quick to pick Interior Decoration on her day. Turns out she has a real knack for making any home feel more cosy and more deadly.

I, personally, would never have thought to use an old skull as a flower vase. That takes skill.

POISON.

THESE PLANTS CAN KILL.

GHOST PEPPER ☐

FERAL FUNGI ☐

☑

☐

MISTLE TOE

SPIKE

Finally, when her turn rolled around, Emmy LouLou headed straight for the Plant Identification badge. We spent the whole day tearing through the swamps. Miss Sage was so pleased with our finds. The Sisters spent the night humming a funeral dirge as they re-stocked the poison pantry.

Everything was perfect as pie,

until it wasn't.

chapter eleven

LET
SLEEPING CAMP
COUNSELLORS
LIE

We were going through our normal morning stretches when I noticed that something was wrong.

I shared a worried look with Emmy LouLou before saying,

 80

"Ma'ams, how bout we get y'all a nice strong cup of coffee, I'll even put in a little eye of newt for that extra zing."

"Oh sugar," slurred Miss Parsleigh. "Hush and shush, and shush hush. I'll wake up any—"

She did not wake up 'any—'. Firstly, because that is an incomplete sentence so it would be impossible to do. Secondly, 'cause she had fallen solidly asleep.

In fact, by the time we got ourselves to the edge of the bayou to start our new badge, Swimming Skills, Miss Parsleigh was snoring. Chainsaw style.

"Don't mind her, she's finer than a June bug in May," fake-laughed Miss Sage in a way that convinced zero of us. "Plus, you got me and Miss Rosemarie – and we are full of energy and ready to go!"

Mary, ever the tactful one, asked, "Does 'full of energy' mean something different in this country? If not, I would guess a more accurate phrase would be 'full of exhaustion and sickness'."

"Sickness, pshaw!" mumbled a cross-eyed Miss Rosemarie. "We are burning precious daylight gabbing,

when we could be swimming. Now, can any of you fine ghouls tell me why it is essential to wait thirty minutes after eating before going for a swim?"

I started jumping up and down. Grams taught me this one when I was a baby. "It's 'cause some people get food cramps, and it might make them drown. And if we drown, we won't earn our Swimming Skills badge."

As soon as I finished talking, I could tell from everybody's faces that I was maybe not right. (Well, everybody except Miss Sage who had joined Miss Parsleigh in an untimely snooze-fest.)

Just then, a tiny little
squeaky voice piped in,
"Kraken!"

Lawdy-loo, Sweet Boo had
talked!

"What on this
green earth is a
Kraken?" I
asked. I was
getting very used to
being the clueless one
around here.

"Ain't you never heard of Dave the
Kraken of Dead Man's Bayou?" scoffed
Bébé.

"Not to worry, Lexie. We got our

very own friendly neighbourhood Kraken. Mind you, Dave wouldn't eat no camper on purpose, he is a true sssss-sss-southern gentleman." Miss Rosemarie paused, her tongue seemed too heavy for talking much. "How . . . However, he is getting on in years and between the blindness and the swamp muck . . . if you smell like a snack, you just might . . . you just . . . well, you just . . . Look, he might just eat you . . ."

And as the words left her mouth, Miss Rosemarie slumped to the ground.

All three sisters were unnaturally fast asleep.

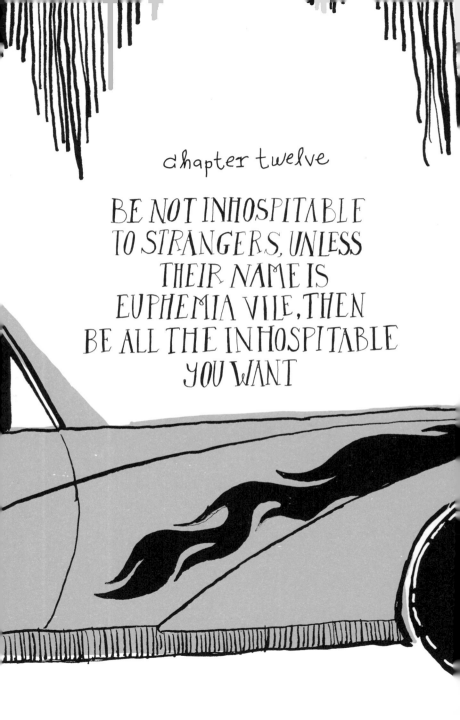

chapter twelve

BE NOT INHOSPITABLE TO STRANGERS, UNLESS THEIR NAME IS EUPHEMIA VILE, THEN BE ALL THE INHOSPITABLE YOU WANT

Before we could even grab them a pillow, a sick-sunshine convertible squealed into camp and a woman with hair bigger than the state of Texas slithered out.

"Oh my word, you poor little lambs!" She bent over, and got right up in my face handing me her business card.

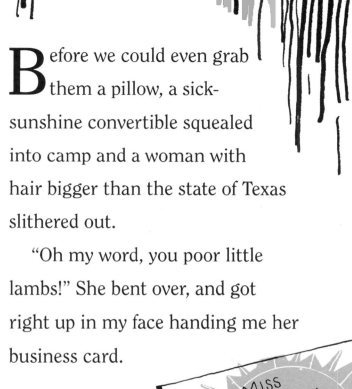

MISS
Euphemia
Vile
SCOUTMASTER
SUPREME*
*the happy hollow camp
for joyful boys
and girls

"I came here last night to have a little chat with the Sisters, and I could tell something was *terribly* wrong. So I thought, being the angel of kindness that I am, I'd show back up this morning, *just in case*. Silly me, I didn't even think to come wearing black. Who would have thought that they'd up and die so quickly?" She winked

one ginormous eyelash at us.

Die? This Vile woman was missing
a puzzle piece in her head! I could still
hear Miss Parsleigh snoring, there was
no way they were dead.

"Well, let's not waste time!" this
human bulldozer hollered. "Y'all can
just go ahead and roll this thing right
into the swamp." Cheerily she pointed
a long pink nail at Miss Parsleigh, Miss
Sage and Miss Rosemarie.

What the heck kind of stranger just
shows up and starts rolling decent
folks into swamps? (Well, other than
Sweet Boo. Her and Kraken Dave are
real close so she'll bring him nibbles

from time to time. That being said, I'm ninety-eight percent sure she wouldn't feed him someone we all love.)

"Shoot, do you have grits for brains or what, sugar?" Bébé hollered as she jumped to protect our snoozing pals.

"We ain't throwing the Sisters into anything but they own bed. Don't make me call my daddy on you.

He don't like it when I get upset, and you won't like it neither – trust me, lady."

If there was a scale for when stuff starts feeling out of control that went from *stubbed toe* to *the airplane I am flying in has run out of jet fuel and we are plunging to our deaths*, I would say this situation was hitting peak *my seatbelt just came unclicked on this rollercoaster.* Time to intervene.

I put on my fake nice-calm-talker voice. Adults respond better when you sound calm.

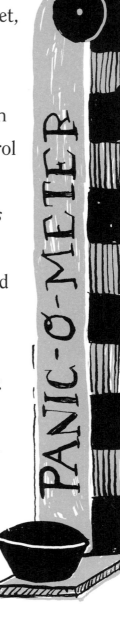

"She don't mean to be rude, ma'am." I did not feel comfortable with the ice stare this woman was giving Bébé, or the one Bébé was giving back for that matter. "But holy guacamole, they are ASLEEP, as in NOT DEAD!" I said the words ASLEEP and NOT DEAD real firm, just to show the lady I knew what I was talking about.

The lady's eyes narrowed, and her lips made a sour twist. "Now, being an extremely polite person, I am not

one to speak ill of the dead or asleep or whatever, but I can see that these counsellors of yours never bothered to teach you lot no manners. There is only one solution. From here on out, you shall refer to me as Scoutmaster Vile, 'cause I'm taking charge."

"Dadgummit," whispered Sweet Boo.

Amen, Sweet Boo, *aaaamen*. Where is a good poking stick when you need one? I'd much rather hang out with the cannibals than this ****.

(Look, I would use a cuss word here, but my Grams raised me to choose my out-loud words wisely. So, I just thought the word inside my head instead. I thought it real hard.)

chapter thirteen

BLESS YOUR SLIMY SAD EXCUSE FOR A HEART

Grams used to tell me, "Sometimes things have to get worse before they get better." Next time I see her, we are going to have a little chit-chat because what's a girl to do if things get worse before they get worser?

Firstly, this Scoutmaster Vile
replaced our uniforms.

There is nothing wrong with being
girly, but what kind of fool wears
Sunday best in a swamp?

Secondly, we lost another friend to the Sleeping Sickness. Nothing and I mean NOTHING could wake Bébé up.

Thirdly and worstly, Scoutmaster Vile was on a badge-earning rampage. In one afternoon we earned at least a bajillion useless badges.

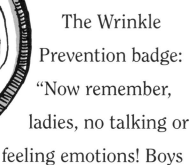

The Wrinkle Prevention badge: "Now remember, ladies, no talking or feeling emotions! Boys hate it when you talk too much anyways, it makes you look less pretty!"

The Helping Hands badge: "Don't forget to massage my toes when you are done down there, pumpkin!"

The Negative Affirmation badge:
"Repeat after me, Scouts, I will never
be as pretty as Scoutmaster Vile.
I will never be as smart as
Scoutmaster Vile. I will never be . . ."

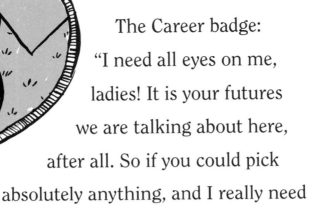

The Career badge:
"I need all eyes on me,
ladies! It is your futures
we are talking about here,
after all. So if you could pick
absolutely anything, and I really need
you to reach for the
stars here – what
career would
you want
your future
husband
to have?"

The Makeover badge: "It's not my fault that some people just can't be helped! Trust me, it's better this way."

chapter fourteen

MAKE LIKE A CHICKEN AND HATCH A PLAN

Emmy LouLou started to cry under her paper bag as we walked to our cabin that night. She had gone back completely whole human, not a whisker in sight, which is never a good sign.

I didn't blame her, not one bit.

On top of feeling totally humiliated and covered in toenail clippings, Scoutmaster Vile's parting words were ringing in my ears: "I had no idea that

fixing you lot would be so gosh darn exhausting. I just hope that all y'all figure out some way to show me just how much you appreciate the hard work I'm doing. After all, Sweet Boo is looking a teensy bit tired. It would be so sad if she joined the sick list and didn't wake up tomorrow . . ."

I was so stuck in my own worries, I didn't notice the monster tree root smack dab in front of my foot. Me and what was left of my dignity soared through the air, and landed in a flump pile of crumpled paper bag and stinging knees.

I could feel my face getting all hot, and a lump of sadness climbing up my throat. I was trying to flatten out the wrinkles in my rotten makeover bag so that nobody would notice I was crying, when I spotted a tiny piece of paper accidentally jammed to the inside.

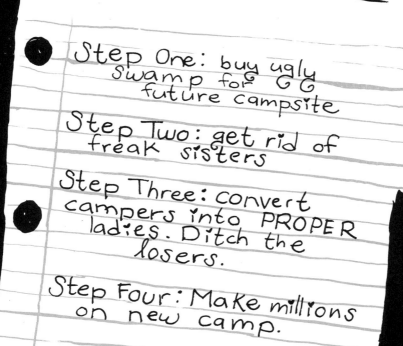

Step One: buy ugly swamp for GG future campsite

Step Two: get rid of freak sisters

Step Three: convert campers into PROPER ladies. Ditch the losers.

Step Four: Make millions on new camp.

And let me tell you what, the words written down on that tiny piece of paper turned my lump of sadness into a sharp box of anger.

HOLY CROW! Scoutmaster Vile wasn't just a little bit evil, she was whole hog *mwahahahaha* evil. I will be darned to heck before I let her hurt any more of my friends.

Maybe Grams could help . . .

The image of her whupping Scoutmaster Vile with that hot pink pleather purse of hers did spring rather quickly to mind. I know, I know. A good purse-smacking doesn't *solve* any problems, but that don't mean I can't enjoy thinking about it.

Alright, fine. Serious mode. What would Grams actually do if she were here?

That wonderful lady would say, "I love you no matter what. Breathe slowly, sugar, and count the facts around you."

FACT No 1 Scoutmaster Vile needs to be taught a serious lesson.

 **FACT No 2** My face is glo-ri-ous. If ANYBODY tries to make me wear a paper bag over it again, I will go full-on human paper shredder. You best believe that bag will get ripped into teensy bits and thrown back in their faces.

 **FACT No 3** We did actually learn a lot of things when the Sisters were teaching us. We even made friends with all them dead folks using the Ouija board!

And suddenly, a beautiful plan blossomed in my brain. A plan so beautiful that if it had a smell, that smell would be fresh chocolate brownies coming out of the oven.

I sprinted to catch up with the others and tell them all about my geniusness. When I was done blabbering, Sweet Boo softly smiled and whispered one tiny, important word: "Revenge!"

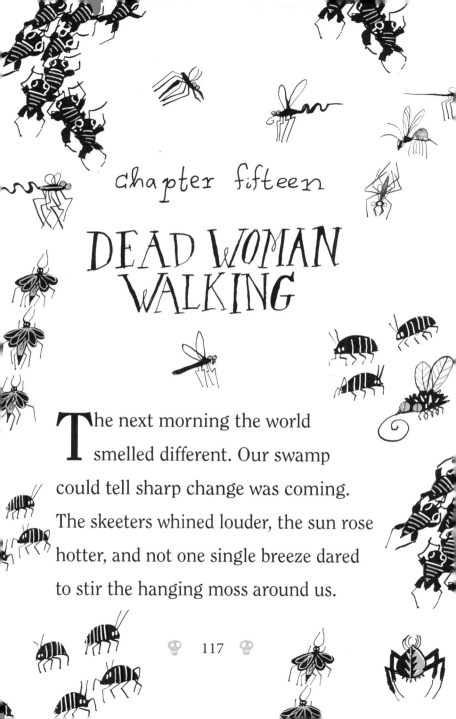

chapter fifteen

DEAD WOMAN WALKING

The next morning the world smelled different. Our swamp could tell sharp change was coming. The skeeters whined louder, the sun rose hotter, and not one single breeze dared to stir the hanging moss around us.

"Good morning, Scouts," Scoutmaster Vile huffed out. She was jumpy, I could see it in the hummingbird-speed wave of her paper fan.

"Good morning, Scoutmaster Vile," we droned in perfect unison, smiling just like she taught us.

"Did no one think to put on some make-up before coming out in public?" She tittered. The peach fuzz on her upper lip

was gathering a sweat moustache. "Y'all are starting to look like a bunch of drowned rats."

Time to get this ball rolling.

"Dearest Scoutmaster," I proclaimed. "Sweet Boo is running herself a fever this morning, so she won't be joining in on the festivities today but – SURPRISE! – we are throwing a 'thank you for helping us even though we are garbage people' party, just for you!" I pointed at the balloons and silly string around us.

Interior Decoration badge: check!
Bébé would be so proud.

Emmy LouLou was next up. I could
see, plain as the nose on my face,
she was terrified. Those anxiety bald
patches were popping up all over her
arms. Nevertheless, she persisted and
stepped forward.

"I . . . I . . . sewed and lint-rollered
this cape in your honour. It is an exact

replica of the one Marie Antoinette wore right before she got her head chopped off. Fit for a queen," she whispered before handing it over.

Needlecraft badge: check!

"Now this is more like it!" Scoutmaster Vile hummed in delight as she flicked a little patch of fur off the collar. "What else have you precious dumplings got for me?"

Her eyes glinted greedily, as Mary took the spotlight.

"Did you know that

mint-chocolate-chip ice cream is the most popular flavour sold in the average American supermarket during the summer season? I made this bowl for you by hand."

And cool as a cucumber, Mary slid that beautiful bowl right into Scoutmaster Vile's claws. She started shovelling that ice cream into her face faster than a hog on a diet.

"As for me, I have no gifts to offer, other than to keep you entertained while you chow down." I bowed grandly. "May I present to you, a story of my own creation.

Once upon a time there was a beautiful queen named Euphemia. She had money. She had a pretty face. She had a talent for making people cry. So pretty, so nice, so gifted.

The whole kingdom wanted to be just like her."

I could see a dribble of ice cream worming its way down her chin as she continued eating and nodding along with my story.

"Except that's not true, is it?" I looked Scoutmaster Vile dead in the eyes and just before I flicked the mega light switch, I could sense her first moment of doubt. "My Grams always says if you cover dog poo in glitter, it's still just dog poo. And Queen Euphemia was a GIANT stinking hot pile of glittering poo."

Watching Euphemia Vile's face flip from doubt to rage was as beautiful as any Fourth of July fireworks display. I could hear teeth grinding and nostrils flaring, she was that mad at us. She rocketed up out of her chair.

I carried on. "Hold your horses, Scoutmaster Vile, my story ain't finished yet! Now, where was I? Oh,

yes – there was a giant pile of poo that had just gone and polished off a pint of ice cream. What the poo didn't know, was that the ice cream was filled with thirteen ghost peppers and a bucket of beetle legs. Say, Mary, don't you have a fun fact about ghost peppers?"

"Why, yes, Lexie, I rather think I do," said Mary sweetly. "Did you know that the ghost pepper is considered the deadliest plant in the world? If you don't drink a gallon of milk or water immediately, it will quite literally burn you up from the inside out."

I love that girl and her helpful facts. Plant Identification badge: check!

Scoutmaster Vile sprinted faster than a feral cat for the fridge. A fridge that we had stocked up only that morning with yet another surprise.

Pen Pal badge: check!

And then, for our grand finale,
Sweet Boo made her utterly
unforgettable fiery entrance.
"For Bébé!" she screamed.
Fire Safety badge: check! ✔

With that, Euphemia Vile officially
(but sadly, not literally) lost her head.

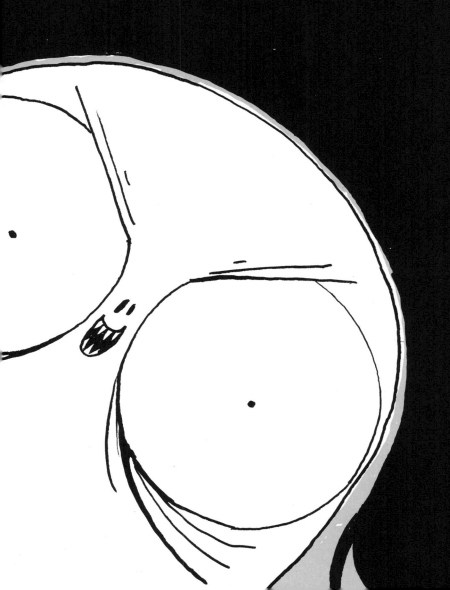

chapter sixteen

REVENGE IS A DISH BEST SERVED SPICY

At lightning speed, Scoutmaster Vile booked it out the door and swan-dived into the only body of water for miles around. With a giant *KERSPLASH* and a *HISSSSS* of steaming clothes, she ended up wallowing in the middle of Dead Man's Bayou.

"You repulsive, sweaty little worms!" she spat out. "This camp is MINE! I aim to sell all y'all to the circus, so I can fill this place up with beautiful rich people who *appreciate* me! Ohohoho, all except you, Miss Thang . . ." She directed her ghost-

pepper-fuelled rage at me. "I have something extra special for *you!* Have you noticed just how many jars full of diseases happen to totally-not-on-purpose lose their lids? Just one tiny slip of the wrist and you'll be—"

"Oh my word, let me tell you what – that some good eatin' there!" Kraken Dave smacked his enormous lips together oh-so-happily. "I love me some tabasco sauce kinda spice, but that was something I ain't never had before! Boy, snackings sure don't get no better than that."

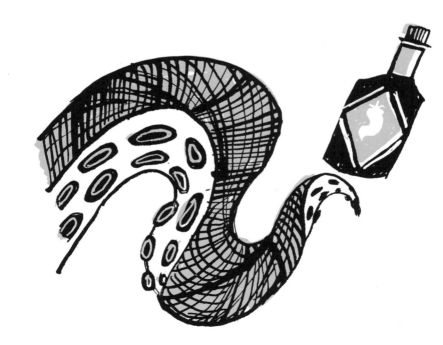

And with a wink he sank back beneath the surface. Taking with him all our stress, our pointless badges, and 162 pounds of nasty. (And if you think I'm talking about Kraken Dave there, you need to think about that one more time.)

"Did y'all go an' throw a party without inviting us?" broke in a sleepy but wonderfully familiar voice.

JOY OF JOYS!

I guess even a serious illness can't keep a Ghoul Scout down for long, because Miss Parsleigh, Miss Sage, Miss Rosemarie AND Bébé were stiffly walking our way. In under two seconds, we pounced on them. I don't think I have ever been in a happier crowd of hugs and laughter.

"Of course we wouldn't have a party without y'all!" I squeaked out from under the wonderful squish of my friends. "We was just doing a little house cleaning, some pesky vermin needed exterminating."

I was warm-toes-warm-heart kind of happy.

Everything was good in the world.

(Or at least, everything should have been. If only we had known that poor Kraken Dave sometimes suffers from indigestion. Indigestion that is not helped when your meal is kicking you from the inside.)

"I'LL GET YOU, MY UGLIES, AND YOUR LITTLE CAMP TOO!"

GLOSSARY

A helpful section in any book that most people skip over, but you shouldn't.

Baron Samedi: the head Loa (spirit, see Loa below) of the Ghede family, and a master of the dead, guardian of cemeteries and linked to magic.

Bayou: a marshy, slow-moving swamp river area, home to alligators, wild pigs, poisonous water snakes, and all kinds of bugs.

Cajun: the Cajuns, also known as Acadians, are an ethnic group living in Louisiana. Descended from French

immigrants driven out of Nova Scotia,
this is a culture famous for their crawfish
boils, brilliant accents that actors rarely
get right in movies, and swamp tours.

Chupacabra: Puerto Rican monsters
with a name that literally translates to
goat-sucker, as they are known to suck
out all the blood from goats like they are
sipping on a juice box.

Dadgummit: a nice way of saying a
certain swear word.

Dolly Parton: a country music
singer-songwriter, actress and all
around fabulous human. She once said,
"Figure out who you are and do it on

purpose" which seems like a pretty solid way to live.

Grits: a cornmeal porridge eaten mostly in the southern parts of the United States that can be paired with sweet (brown sugar) or savoury (shrimp and gravy) toppings.

Gumbo: a big ol' pot of yum common in southern Louisiana. There is a big difference between Cajun Gumbo and Creole Gumbo, so try both if you ever end up in Louisiana yourself! This dish always has a base of celery, onions and bell peppers, but after that it's a free-for-all depending on the area and

family recipe traditions.

Hades: the Greek god of the dead and King of the Underworld.

Loa: the spirits of Louisiana Voodoo. While they are not gods themselves, they are treated with great respect and served in the hopes that the Loa will convey their prayers to God.

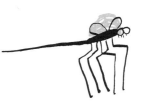

Louisiana Creole: Louisiana folks who have colonial French, colonial Spanish, African American or Native American ancestry. This is a culture famous for its amazing food, the creation of Zydeco music, and over 100 Creole languages.

Louisiana Voodoo (also called New Orleans Voodoo): an Afro-American religion rooted in West African Vodun, brought over to Louisiana during the height of the atrocious transatlantic slave trade. This religion has many overlapping elements (and is sometimes confused) with Hoodoo, Catholicism and Haitian Vodou.

Marie Antoinette: the Queen of France during the French Revolution, painted wearing some fabulous dresses and froufrou wigs.

Ouija Board: spirit board used by the living to contact the dead.

Skeeters: mosquitoes. Real-life bug monsters that love making my skin itch.

Snatcher: a team member when playing "How to Catch a Cold". Their job is to run after the blobs and catch them with their butterfly nets.

Sneezer: a team member when playing "How to Catch a Cold" whose task it is to lure in blobs by pretending to be very, very sick. The more drama, the better.

Tabasco Sauce: a brand of hot sauce that goes real good on a whole range of foods. I personally recommend trying some on your morning eggs.

GHOUL SCOUT EXTRAS

1. Ghoul Scout hand sign:

Raise your paws and show some claws!

2. Ghoul Scout pledge:

On my dishonour, I will try:

to serve whoever or whatever suits me,

to help the living and the dead at all

times, and to live by the Ghoul

Scout Law.

3. Ghoul Scout Law:

I will do my best to be

honest and fair,

friendly-ish and helpful,

considerate and caring,

brush my fangs and shower occasionally,

be responsible for what I say and do,

and to

respect myself because I am awesome,

respect authority when they have earned

my respect,

use resources wisely,

make the world a stranger place,

and be a sibling to every Ghoul Scout.

 153

BIOGRAPHY:

Taylor Dolan was born into a house of stories and raised in Texas. Her mother used to read to her every night, and together they made their way through the worlds of Narnia, Oz and many more. Sometimes, when Taylor is feeling blue, her mother still reads to her and does the best voices for all the characters.

When she was younger she was a proud Girl Scout in Troop 809. During that time, she sold (and ate) many Girl Scout Cookies, camped down the street from an Emu farm, and learned the painful fish-flop method of re-entering a canoe after having been pushed in the water.

Many years later, she attended the Cambridge School of Art for her Master's Degree in Children's Book Illustration. She now lives in Arkansas, while using her imagination to pretend she still lives in Cambridge. This is her first written and illustrated book, and contains many little pieces of her heart.